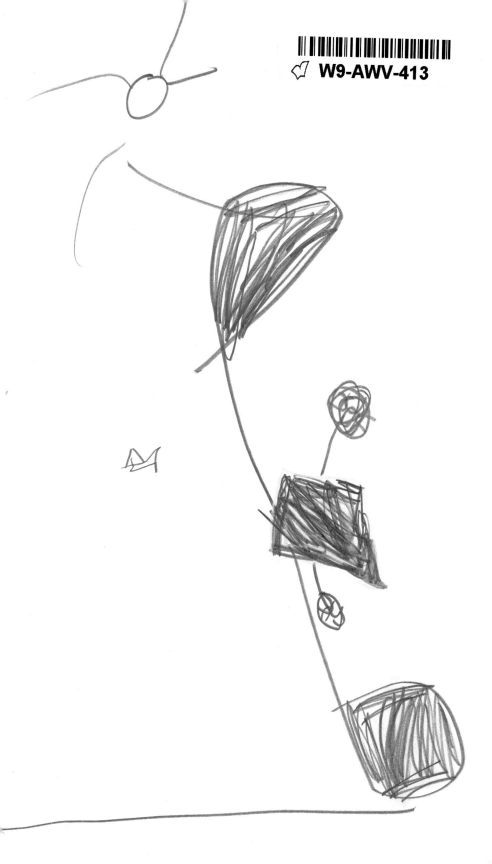

Dear Parent:

Remember the first time you read a book by yourself? I do.
I still remember the thrill of reading the words Little Bear said
to Mother Bear: "I have a new space helmet. I am going to
the moon."

Later when my daughter was
learning to read, her favorite I
Can Read books were the funny
ones—Danny playing with the
dinosaur he met at the museum
and Amelia Bedelia dressing
the chicken. And now as a new
teacher, she has joined the
thousands of teachers who use
I Can Read books in the classroom.

I'm delighted to share this commemorative edition with you.
This special volume includes the origin stories and early sketches
of many beloved I Can Read characters.

Here's to the next sixty years—and to all those beginning
readers who are about to embark on a lifetime of discovery that
starts with the magical words *"I can read!"*

Kate M. Jackson
Senior VP, Associate Publisher, Editor-in-Chief

I Can Read!

READING 2 WITH HELP

Amelia Bedelia

by Peggy Parish

pictures by Fritz Siebel

HarperCollins*Publishers*

Amelia Bedelia
Text copyright © 1963 by Margaret Parish. Text copyright renewed 1991 by the Estate of Margaret Parish. Illustrations copyright © 1963 by Fritz Siebel. Illustrations copyright renewed 1991 by the Estate of Fritz Siebel. Revised illustrations copyright © 1992 by the Estate of Fritz Siebel. Amelia Bedelia is a registered trademark of Peppermint Partners, LLC.
Illustration on page 1 copyright © 1963 by Fritz Siebel; renewed 1992 by the Estate of Fritz Siebel.
Additional illustrations on pages 68–71: Amelia Bedelia sketch copyright © 2013 by the Estate of Fritz Siebel from *Amelia Bedelia: Fiftieth Anniversary Edition*. Berenstain Bears sketch copyright © 2017 by Berenstain Bears, Inc. Biscuit sketch copyright © 2017 by Pat Schories. Danny and the Dinosaur sketch copyright © 2017 by Anti-Defamation League Foundation, Inc., The Author's Guild Foundation, Inc., ORT America, Inc., United Negro College Fund, Inc. Fancy Nancy sketch copyright © 2017 by Robin Preiss Glasser. Frog and Toad sketch copyright © 2017 by the Estate of Arnold Lobel. Little Critter sketch copyright © 2017 by Mercer Mayer. Pete the Cat sketch copyright © 2017 by James Dean. Pinkalicious sketch copyright © 2017 by Victoria Kann. All rights reserved. Manufactured in China. No part of this book may be used or reproduced in any manner whatsoever without written permission except in the case of brief quotations embodied in critical articles and reviews. For information address HarperCollins Children's Books, a division of HarperCollins Publishers, 195 Broadway, New York, NY 10007. www.icanread.com

Library of Congress Cataloging-in-Publication Data
Parish, Peggy.
    Amelia Bedelia / by Peggy Parish ; pictures by Fritz Siebel. — New ed.
        p. cm. — (An I can read book)
    Summary: A literal-minded housekeeper causes a ruckus in the household when she attempts to make sense of some instructions.
    ISBN 978-0-06-257279-0 (pob.)
    [1. Humorous stories.] I. Siebel, Fritz, ill. II. Title. III. Series.
PZ7.P219Am 1992   91-10163
[E]—dc20   CIP
                                                                                                  AC

17 18 19 20 21 SCP 10 9 8 7 6 5 4 3 2 1   ❖   Originally published in 1963

For Debbie, John Grier,
Walter, and Michael Dinkins

"Oh, Amelia Bedelia,
your first day of work,
and I can't be here.
But I made a list for you.
You do just what the list says,"
said Mrs. Rogers.
Mrs. Rogers got into the car
with Mr. Rogers.
They drove away.

"My, what nice folks.

I'm going to like working here,"

said Amelia Bedelia.

9

Amelia Bedelia went inside.

"Such a grand house.

These must be rich folks.

But I must get to work.

Here I stand just looking.

And me with a whole list

of things to do."

Amelia Bedelia stood there

a minute longer.

"I think I'll make

a surprise for them.

I'll make lemon-meringue pie.

I do make good pies."

So Amelia Bedelia went
into the kitchen.
She put a little of this
and a pinch of that
into a bowl.
She mixed and she rolled.

Soon her pie was ready

to go into the oven.

"There," said Amelia Bedelia.

"That's done."

"Now let's see what this list says."

Amelia Bedelia read,

Change the towels in the green bathroom.

Amelia Bedelia found

the green bathroom.

"Those towels are very nice.

Why change them?" she thought.

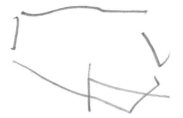

Then Amelia Bedelia remembered

what Mrs. Rogers had said.

She must do just what

the list told her.

"Well, all right,"

said Amelia Bedelia.

Amelia Bedelia got some scissors.

She snipped a little here

and a little there.

And she changed those towels.

"There," said Amelia Bedelia.

She looked at her list again.

Dust the furniture.

"Did you ever hear tell

of such a silly thing.

At my house we undust the furniture.

But to each his own way."

Amelia Bedelia took
one last look at the bathroom.
She saw a big box with the words
Dusting Powder on it.

"Well, look at that.

A special powder to dust with!"

exclaimed Amelia Bedelia.

So Amelia Bedelia

dusted the furniture.

"That should be dusty enough.

My, how nice it smells."

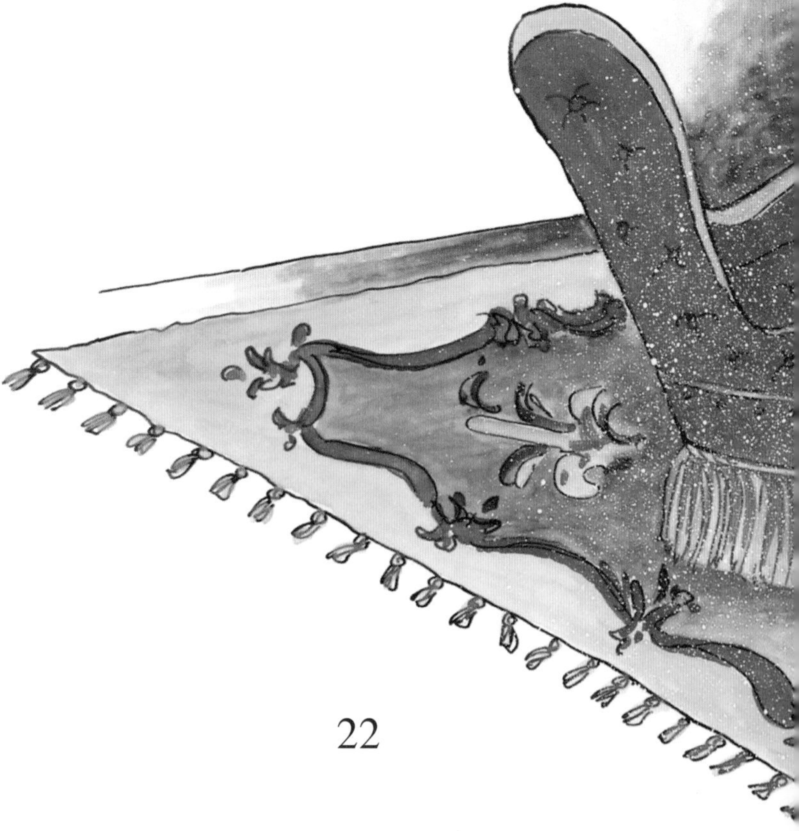

Draw the drapes when the sun comes in.

read Amelia Bedelia.

She looked up.

The sun was coming in.

Amelia Bedelia looked

at the list again.

"Draw the drapes?

That's what it says.

I'm not much

of a hand at drawing,

but I'll try."

25

So Amelia Bedelia sat right down
and she drew those drapes.

Amelia Bedelia

marked off

about the drapes.

"Now what?"

Put the lights out when you
finish in the living room.

Amelia Bedelia
thought about this a minute.
She switched off the lights.
Then she carefully
unscrewed each bulb.

And Amelia Bedelia
put the lights out.
"So those things need
to be aired out, too.
Just like pillows and babies.
Oh, I do have a lot to learn."

"My pie!" exclaimed Amelia Bedelia.

She hurried to the kitchen.

"Just right," she said.

She took the pie out of the oven

and put it on the table to cool.

Then she looked at the list.

Measure two cups of rice.

"That's next," said Amelia Bedelia.

Amelia Bedelia found two cups.

She filled them with rice.

And Amelia Bedelia

measured that rice.

Amelia Bedelia laughed.

"These folks

do want me to do funny things."

Then she poured the rice

back into the container.

The meat market will deliver a steak and a chicken.

Please trim the fat before you put the steak in the icebox.

And please dress the chicken.

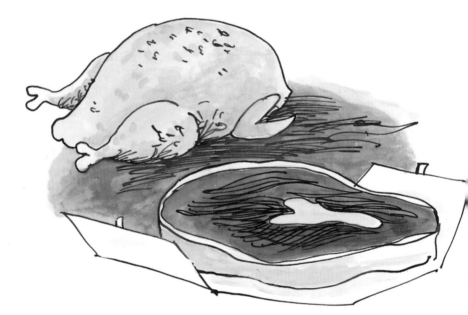

When the meat arrived,

Amelia Bedelia opened the bag.

She looked at the steak

for a long time.

"Yes," she said.

"That will do nicely."

Amelia Bedelia got some lace

and bits of ribbon.

And Amelia Bedelia

trimmed that fat

before she put

the steak in the icebox.

"Now I must dress the chicken.

I wonder if she wants

a he chicken or a she chicken?"

said Amelia Bedelia.

Amelia Bedelia went right to work.

Soon the chicken was finished.

Amelia Bedelia heard the door open.

"The folks are back," she said.

She rushed out to meet them.

"Amelia Bedelia,

why are all the light bulbs outside?"

asked Mr. Rogers.

"The list just said

to put the lights out,"

said Amelia Bedelia.

"It didn't say to bring them back in.

Oh, I do hope

they didn't get aired too long."

"Amelia Bedelia,

the sun will fade the furniture.

I asked you to draw the drapes,"

said Mrs. Rogers.

"I did! I did! See,"

said Amelia Bedelia.

She held up her picture.

Then Mrs. Rogers saw the furniture.

"The furniture!" she cried.

"Did I dust it well enough?"

asked Amelia Bedelia.

"That's such nice dusting powder."

Mr. Rogers went to wash his hands.

"I say," he called.

"These are very unusual towels."

Mrs. Rogers dashed into the bathroom.

"Oh, my best towels," she said.

"Didn't I change them enough?"

asked Amelia Bedelia.

53

Mrs. Rogers went to the kitchen.

"I'll cook the dinner.

Where is the rice

I asked you to measure?"

"I put it back in the container.

But I remember—

it measured four and a half inches,"

said Amelia Bedelia.

"Was the meat delivered?"

asked Mrs. Rogers.

"Yes," said Amelia Bedelia.

"I trimmed the fat just like you said.

It does look nice."

Mrs. Rogers rushed to the icebox.

She opened it.

"Lace! Ribbons!

Oh, dear!" said Mrs. Rogers.

"The chicken—you dressed

the chicken?"

asked Mrs. Rogers.

"Yes, and I found the nicest box

to put him in,"

said Amelia Bedelia.

"Box!" exclaimed Mrs. Rogers.

Mrs. Rogers hurried over to the box.

She lifted the lid.

There lay the chicken.

And he was just as dressed

as he could be.

Mrs. Rogers was angry.

She was very angry.

She opened her mouth.

Mrs. Rogers meant

to tell Amelia Bedelia

she was fired.

But before she could

get the words out,

Mr. Rogers put something

in her mouth.

It was so good

Mrs. Rogers forgot about being angry.

"Lemon-meringue pie!"

she exclaimed.

"I made it to surprise you,"

said Amelia Bedelia happily.

So right then and there

Mr. and Mrs. Rogers decided

that Amelia Bedelia must stay.

And so she did.

Mrs. Rogers learned to say

undust the furniture,

unlight the lights,

close the drapes,

and things like that.

Mr. Rogers didn't care

if Amelia Bedelia

trimmed all

of his steaks with lace.

All he cared about

was having her there

to make lemon-meringue pie.

"I can read! I can read!
Where are the books for me?"

One question from a young reader sparked a reading revolution!

A conversation between the director of Harper's Department of Books for Boys and Girls, Ursula Nordstrom, and Boston Public Library's Virginia Haviland inspired the I Can Read book series. Haviland told Nordstrom that a young boy had burst into the children's reading room and asked her where he could find books that were just right for a brand-new reader like himself.

Determined to fill this gap, Nordstrom published *Little Bear* by Else Holmelund Minarik, with illustrations by Maurice Sendak, in the fall of 1957. The response was immediate. According to the *New York Times*, "One look at the illustrations and children will grab for it. A second look at the short, easy sentences, the repetition of words, and the beautiful type spacing, and children will know they can read it themselves."

Delightful and wonderfully warm, *Little Bear* served as the template for the series, and now, sixty years later, we have over four hundred I Can Read stories for our youngest and newest readers!

Where the Ideas for the Characters Came From

Berenstain Bears

Stan and Jan Berenstain were cartoonists in the 1950s. When their sons began to read, they submitted a story about a family of bears to author, editor, and publisher Ted Geisel (aka Dr. Seuss), which was published as *The Big Honey Hunt* in 1962. Geisel labeled their next effort "Another Adventure of the Berenstain Bears." That's how the bears got their name!

Biscuit

One day while watching her daughter play with their neighbor's frisky dog, Alyssa Capucilli was struck by her daughter's patience and gentle nature, as well as the fact that her little girl thought the dog understood every word she said. That was the inspiration for the little yellow puppy and his sweet companion. Pat Schories's warm illustrations capture their tender relationship.

Pete the Cat

When James Dean first saw Pete, he was a tiny black kitten in a shelter. Pete looked like he had been starved and his black fur was a mess. At first, James had no interest in Pete—black cats were bad luck, after all! But the scrawny little fellow stuck his paw out of the cage, wanting to play! James took Pete home. And even though James chose to paint Pete the Cat blue (his favorite color), James realizes now that black cats are actually very good luck.

Danny and the Dinosaur

In 1958, cartoonist Syd Hoff's daughter Susan was going through a rough surgery, and one day, Syd decided to draw a picture to cheer her up. It showed a dinosaur with Syd's brother on its back. When Susie saw the picture, she exclaimed, "Danny and the dinosaur!" and that night after the family went to bed, Syd wrote the story.

Pinkalicious

Victoria Kann's daughters could never seem to get enough of cupcakes or the color pink! One year, as an April Fools' joke, Victoria told her family and friends that one of her daughters had turned pink from eating too many pink cupcakes—and so the idea for *Pinkalicious* was born!

Frog and Toad

he characters of Frog and his best friend, Toad, might have been spired by . . . a horror movie! Arnold Lobel and his daughter, Adrianne, ent to see a movie called *Frogs* at the drive-in. However, the movie atured not frogs, but toads! Adrianne told her dad about the many ifferences between the two—and two years later the first Frog and oad book, *Frog and Toad Are Friends*, appeared.

Little Critter

Mercer Mayer was doodling around one day in 1974 when he drew a shape like a gourd, put two eyes on it, scribbled a nose connecting the eyes, then got coffee and forgot about it! The next day, he noticed a small piece of paper on the floor. It was his gourd. He added fuzzy hair and a big mouth; short stubby arms and feet. Mercer had created a fuzzy little "woodchuck-y porcupine" thing that became Little Critter!

Fancy Nancy

Vhen Jane O'Connor was a small girl, every Sunday, when her grandma nd great aunts came to visit, Jane would greet them at the door in tutu and a pair of her mom's high heels. She thought she looked ès glamorous!

Years later, while she was fixing dinner one night, the name Fancy ancy flew into Jane's head, and a star made her debut!

Amelia Bedelia

Amelia Bedelia was inspired by Peggy Parish's third-grade students at the Dalton School in New York City. The children mixed up words, and Parish found them hilarious. That gave Parish the idea for Amelia Bedelia—a character who takes every word literally and embraces life with an outlook that is forthright and optimistic. Illustrator Fritz Siebel worked with Parish to create the perfect look for the conscientious cleaning lady.

Early Character Development

The Berenstain Bears

Stan and Jan Berenstain's early sketches from *The Berenstain Bears Clean House*

Pete the Cat

Frog and Toad
Early character sketch of Frog and Toad

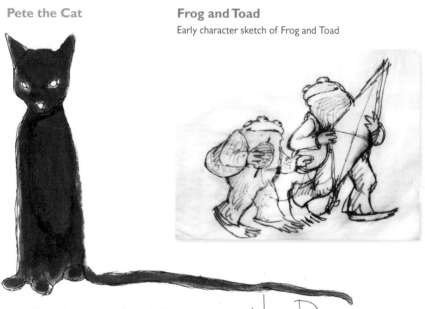

James Dean's first painting of Pete the Cat

JAMES DEAN
12. 26. 99

Biscuit character sketches

Pat Schories's early sketches from *Biscuit*

Pinkalicious

Victoria Kann's sketches for the picture book *Pinkalicious*

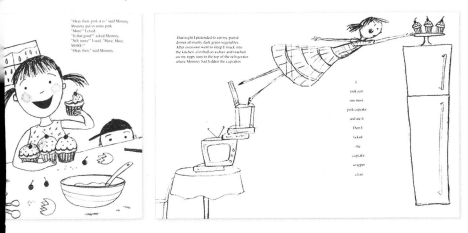

Amelia Bedelia

Fritz Siebel's sketches
for the picture book
Amelia Bedelia

Danny and the Dinosaur

Syd Hoff's early cover sketches for *Danny and the Dinosaur*

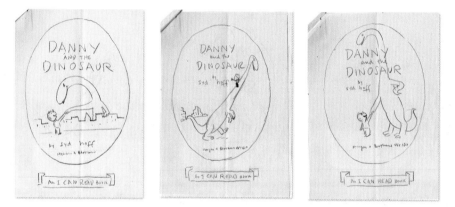

Little Critter

Mercer Mayer's early
character sketches of
Little Critter

obin Preiss Glasser's character sketches and cover sketch for *Fancy Nancy and the Boy from Paris*

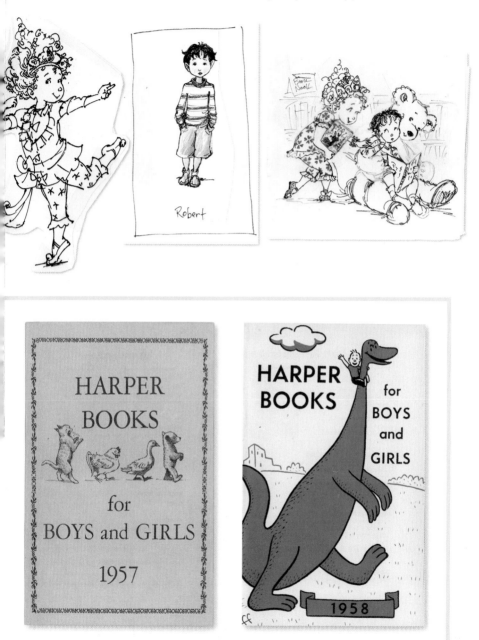

Robert

HARPER
BOOKS

for
BOYS and GIRLS

1957

HARPER
BOOKS
for
BOYS
and
GIRLS

1958

These two catalogs marked the launch of I Can Read!

Sixty Years of I CAN READ

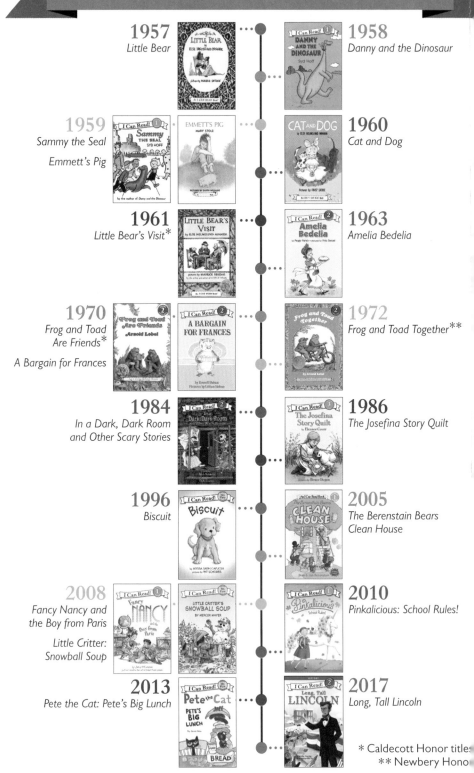

1957 Little Bear

1958 Danny and the Dinosaur

1959 Sammy the Seal / Emmett's Pig

1960 Cat and Dog

1961 Little Bear's Visit*

1963 Amelia Bedelia

1970 Frog and Toad Are Friends* / A Bargain for Frances

1972 Frog and Toad Together**

1984 In a Dark, Dark Room and Other Scary Stories

1986 The Josefina Story Quilt

1996 Biscuit

2005 The Berenstain Bears Clean House

2008 Fancy Nancy and the Boy from Paris / Little Critter: Snowball Soup

2010 Pinkalicious: School Rules!

2013 Pete the Cat: Pete's Big Lunch

2017 Long, Tall Lincoln

* Caldecott Honor titles
** Newbery Honor